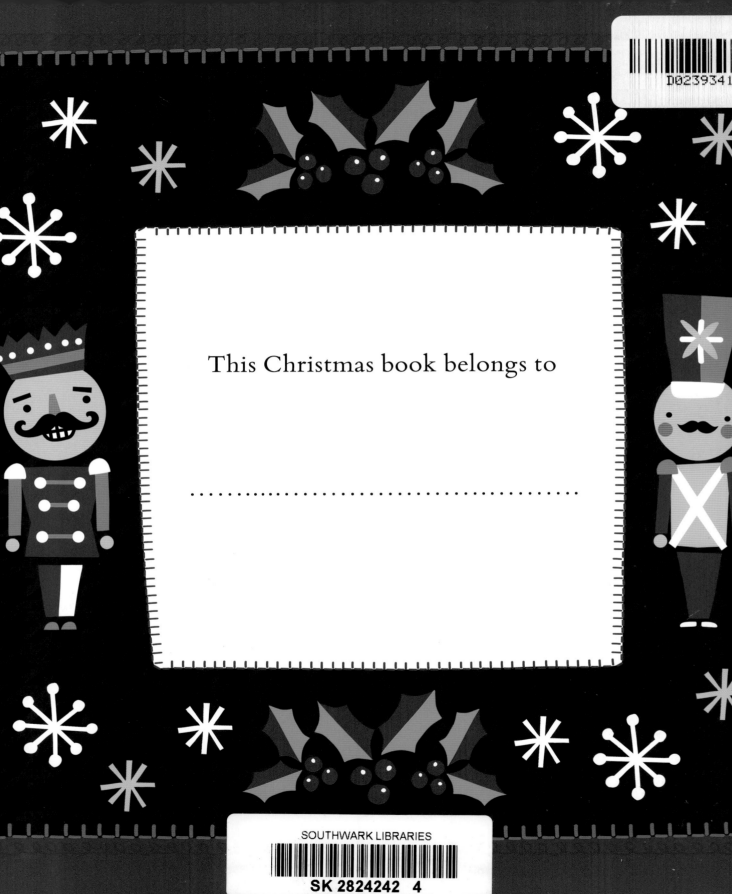

This Christmas book belongs to

....

Peppa Pig

LADYBIRD BOOKS

UK | USA | Canada | Ireland | Australia | India | New Zealand | South Africa

Ladybird Books is part of the Penguin Random House group of companies
whose addresses can be found at global.penguinrandomhouse.com.

www.penguin.co.uk   www.puffin.co.uk   www.ladybird.co.uk

Penguin
Random House
UK

First published 2021
001

Printed in China

entative in the EEA is Penguin Random House Ireland,
ambers, 32 Nassau Street, Dublin D02 YH68

cord for this book is available from the British Library

SBN: 978-0-241-47622-2

All correspondence to:
Books, Penguin Random House Children's
ardens, 8 Viaduct Gardens, London SW11 7BW

Peppa's Christmas Unicorn

It was the beginning of December, and Peppa and her family were decorating their Christmas tree. Peppa pulled a decoration from the Christmas box. "It's the prickly cactus we got when Daddy went monster trucking in America," she cried.

CHRISTMAS DECORATIONS

"And here's the flamingo from our summer holiday!" said Daddy Pig. "What lovely memories," said Mummy Pig, smiling.

"What a perfect tree!" said Daddy Pig, hanging his last bauble. "Hmm, there's still one bare branch."

"But there aren't any decorations left." Peppa sighed. "Never mind," said Mummy Pig. "The tree looks wonderful just as it is!"
"OK," said Peppa. But she couldn't help staring at the empty branch . . .

CHRISTMAS DECORATIONS

A few weeks later, it was Christmas Eve.
"Come on!" called Daddy Pig. "It's time
to go to the Christmas fair."
"Hooray!" cried Peppa and George.

The Christmas fair was lots of fun. There
were stalls full of yummy food, games to play,
gingerbread houses to decorate and . . .

"A Christmas carousel!"
cried Peppa.
"Who wants a ride?"
asked Mummy Pig.
"I do! I do!" cheered
Peppa and George,
jumping up and down.

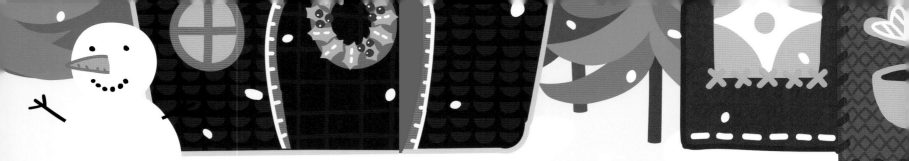

"Daddy Pig," said Mummy Pig, "would you like to ride the carousel?"

Daddy Pig looked at the Christmas carousel. "What does it do?" he asked Miss Rabbit, who was in charge of the ride. "It spins around and around up in the air," she explained.

"Ahh," said Daddy Pig. He was a little bit scared of heights.
"Come on, it'll be so much fun!" said Peppa.
"OK," said Daddy Pig. "I'll give it a whirl!"

Peppa and George looked at all the animals they could ride on the carousel. "Dine-saw! *Grrr!*" shouted George, picking a special Christmas dinosaur. Mummy Pig climbed on the dinosaur with him.

Peppa spotted a golden glittery . . . "Christmas unicorn!" she cried. "I'm riding this one. Doesn't it look magical?" "It certainly does!" agreed Daddy Pig.

"Last call for the magical Christmas carousel!" announced Miss Rabbit. "All aboard!"
"Come on, Daddy!" called Peppa. "Lets hurry!"
Daddy Pig got into Santa's sleigh. "Ho! Ho! Ho!" he cheered.

Once everyone was settled safely on the ride, Miss Rabbit pressed a button. The carousel started to spin around and around, getting faster and faster!
Peppa, George, Mummy and Daddy Pig were lifted up higher and higher up into the air, until suddenly . . .

. . . they were flying!

"Wheeeeeee!" cried Peppa on her magical Christmas unicorn. "Dine-saw! *Grrr!*" cried George on his special Christmas dinosaur. Daddy Pig's sleigh was close behind. His eyes were shut.

"Open your eyes, Daddy!" said Peppa.
"We're flying!"
Daddy Pig opened one eye and looked
down. "Oh my goodness, we **are** flying!"

From up high, Peppa and George could see the houses below decorated with Christmas lights and the trees covered in snow.

"Look, Daddy!" gasped Peppa, pointing. "It's our house!"
Daddy Pig peered down . . . and his sleigh started to drop!
Luckily, Peppa's unicorn helped the reindeer to pull the
sleigh back up again.
"Phew!" said Daddy Pig.

Miss Rabbit pressed a button, and everyone
flew back down to the ground.
"Wasn't that amazing?" cried Peppa.
"We were flying, weren't we, Daddy?"
"It must be Christmas magic," replied
Daddy Pig, a little dizzy from the ride.

"Now, who wants to visit Santa?" asked Mummy Pig.
"I do! I do!" cheered Peppa and George, jumping up and down.

Peppa told Santa all about her magical ride on the flying Christmas unicorn.

"We even saw our house," she cried. "Our Christmas tree was sparkling in the window. We collect decorations!"

"Your tree sounds wonderful!" said Santa.
"I'd love to see it!"
"You can," said Peppa. "Tonight!"
"Oh yes," said Santa. "Of course!"

"I should probably get going," said Santa, chuckling. "I've got rather a busy night of present-delivering ahead of me."
"Yes!" said Peppa excitedly.

"Merry Christmas, Santa!"

"Merry Christmas, Peppa," said Santa.
"It was lovely talking to you!"

"Time to head home," said Mummy Pig.
"It's a big day tomorrow!"

Back at home, Peppa and George got into their cosy
Christmas pyjamas, put out yummy treats for Santa
and his reindeer, and hung up their stockings.

"Please can we have a magical Christmas bedtime story now?" asked Peppa.
Daddy Pig told Peppa and George a magical Christmas bedtime story, and they soon fell fast asleep.

On Christmas morning, Peppa and George
raced downstairs to find that Santa had been.

Peppa peeked into her stocking and pulled out
a little sparkly box. Inside was a glittery golden
Christmas-unicorn tree decoration!
"It's just like the one I rode on the carousel!" she gasped.

"Another lovely memory for the tree," said Mummy Pig.
"And now you have a decoration for that empty branch,"
said Daddy Pig. "Santa is rather clever, isn't he?"

"I love you, Christmas unicorn!"
whispered Peppa.
Suddenly, the unicorn shone brightly
and flew on to the tree branch!
"Wow!" gasped Peppa. "Did you see that?"
"What?" asked Mummy Pig.

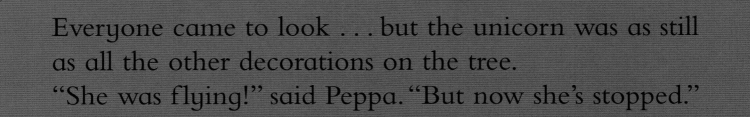

Everyone came to look . . . but the unicorn was as still
as all the other decorations on the tree.
"She was flying!" said Peppa. "But now she's stopped."

"Must be Christmas magic," said Daddy Pig, winking. "Thank you, Santa," Peppa said. "This is the most magical Christmas ever!"

Peppa loves Christmas unicorns.
Everyone loves Christmas unicorns!